Grace the Pirate

by Kathryn Lasky

Illustrated by Karen Lee Schmidt

Hyperion Books for Children
New York

Printed in the United States of America.

First Edition
1 3 5 7 9 10 8 6 4 2

This book is set in 16-point Berkeley.
The artwork for each picture was prepared using pencil.

Library of Congress Cataloging-in-Publication Data

Lasky, Kathryn.
Grace the Pirate / Kathryn Lasky ; illustrated by Karen Lee Schmidt.
p.   cm.
Summary: Grace O'Malley finds excitement and danger when she defies Irish
tradition and goes off to sea with her father, a trader and pirate.
ISBN 0-7868-1147-1 (pbk.)—ISBN 0-7868-2236-8 (lib. bdg.)
1. O'Malley, Grace, 1530?-1603?—Juvenile fiction. [1. O'Malley, Grace,
1530?–1603?—Fiction. 2. Pirates—Fiction. 3. Sex role—Fiction. 4. Ireland—
Fiction. 5. Sea stories.] I. Schmidt, Karen, ill. II. Title.
PZ7.L3274Gr   1997
[Fic]—dc21   97-9947

Contents

1. Grace by the Sea   1

2. Grace the Bald   6

3. To Capture a Star   13

4. Mad Dogs and Merrows   20

5. Grace the Pirate   28

6. Grace in Battle   35

7. Many Years Later—Two Queens Meet   40

Author's Note: The Pirate Queen   47

Grace the Pirate

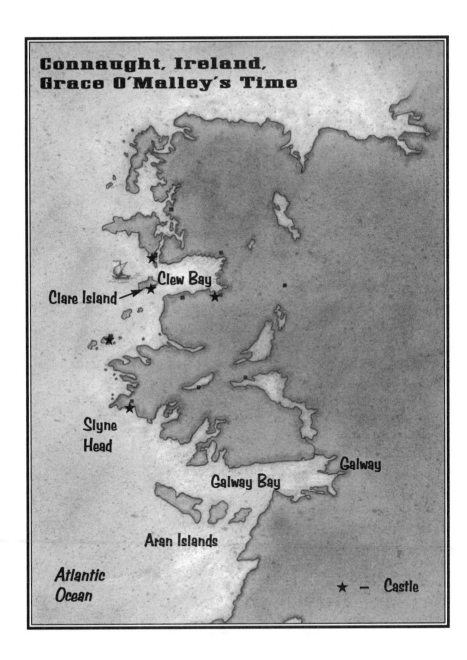

Connaught, Ireland,
Grace O'Malley's Time

Clew Bay

Clare Island

Slyne
Head

Galway

Galway Bay

Aran Islands

Atlantic
Ocean

★ — Castle

Chapter 1

Grace by the Sea

Once upon a time, nearly five hundred years ago, there was a girl named Grace born by the edge of the Atlantic Ocean. Her family, a powerful old clan by the name of O'Malley, ruled lands that stretched to the north, to the south, to the east, and to the west in the countryside known as Connaught in Ireland.

Grace grew up in castles, for there were at least five of them spread across the

O'Malleys' lands. Her favorite castle was on the island of Clare at the head of the bay of Clew. And her favorite place to be was not in the castle, but on one of her father's galley ships. Her father, Owen O'Malley, known as Black Oak, controlled all of Clew Bay and a great part of the sea beyond.

It was from the sea that the O'Malleys made their living. They fished for lobsters, cockles, herring, cod, and crab. They also traded fish and woolens and salt and linens for wine and spices and silk. For these goods they sailed to France and Spain, since the English did not let them trade in the main port city of western Ireland, Galway. When the fishing was no good and the trading was poor, the O'Malleys, like many other Irish clans, turned to piracy. Because the O'Malleys knew the way of the sea better than any other of the clans, they were the best pirates of all.

And that was why, one fine summer

day, Grace was angry. She sat at the table and slurped her hot cereal noisily as she stared out the window. She wanted to be plundering and pirating, not spinning and churning.

"Grace!" her mother called from the spinning wheel for the third time. "Quit staring out the window for your father's sail. He shall be here when he comes—no sooner, no later. There be a westerly wind. He is coming from the east. It's bound to slow him down."

Grace made a face. Her mother knew nothing about sailing. She talked as if it were unusual that there was a westerly wind. There was *always* a westerly wind, and when her father traded he *always* went east to Scotland or south to Spain and France. She dumped another glob of honey in the bowl and scooped up her last handful of cereal. She then wiped her hand on her dress, sniffled loudly, and stomped off toward the second spinning wheel.

Grace picked a puff of wool from the

basket at her mother's feet. She began to blend it into the yarn already on the wheel.

"Your nose is running, dear. Don't drip on the wool."

Grace wiped the snot on her sleeve. Her nose ran only when she was inside, never while she was outside. That was where she belonged, at sea. Grace knew it. She had known it forever. And now that she was almost ten, she planned to do something about it. Her father would not get away again without her. Grace spit on the tail of yarn already on the wheel, pressed some more wool onto it, and stomped on the foot pedal. By Mananan's whiskers, she swore she would get to sea! Whiskers! Whiskers! Whiskers on the chin! Hair on the head! Suddenly Grace had a wonderful idea!

Chapter 2

Grace the Bald

On the north side of the island of Clare the cliffs rose over one thousand feet out of the sea. At the base of the cliffs was a notch where the water rushed in. And deep within the notch, where it was safe and cozy, the water grew still and smooth. Grace knelt at the edge of this pool. She took her knife and began to hack at her long dark hair. Soon she had a handful of hair. She leaned over and looked at herself in the water. "Too long!" she

muttered, and took up the knife again and began to cut more. Soon a soft pile of hair lay around her knees, and tufts drifted on the surface of the pool. She looked once more into the water. She blinked. "Me?" she whispered. A smile broke across her face. She looked like a boy. Her father had to let her sail. He just had to!

She stood up and brushed off the dark curls of hair. She remembered the eagles that nested on the cliffs above. The hair would be perfect for their nest. So she gathered handfuls and stuffed them into the pocket of her smock. On the ground lay the linen headcloth that all girls and women wore on their heads. She stared at it. Should she wear it or not? There was no need. Her hair was so short now, it would never get in her way when she spun or wove or churned butter. She picked up the headcloth and tied it around her waist. For now she would be bareheaded.

Grace followed a path that led up to the top of the cliffs. Just before the top, the path was no wider than a man's foot. She stopped and tucked her undersmock up into her tunic. Now she was ready to climb the last twenty feet. She knew every handhold and foothold.

When she reached the top, the wind whipped around the cliffs and through her short hair. She closed her eyes and grinned. How good the wind felt on her scalp. Looking out to the sea, she saw the white-crested waves that sailors called the horses of Mananan, Lord of the Seas, tossing their manes. She squinted. Was that a sail? Her father coming home? Grace touched the stubble of her hair nervously. Well, it was too late to do anything about it now. An eagle screeched overhead, and Grace remembered why she was there. She put the wads of hair in a bush where they would stay until the eagle found them for its nest.

* * *

Grace stood on the beach. She stood straight and still and looked ahead. She did not flinch as the other children danced around and teased her.

"Grace the Bald! Grace the Bald!
Gave her head a mighty scald!
Cut her hair right to the skin
And now she looks just like a him!"

The galley drew closer as the oarsmen rowed in. Soon they would pull up the oars and the galley would glide up into the sand. Her father stood ready to give the order. He looked straight ahead and did not recognize her. She felt a strange thrill. Was she really that different? She felt the same as always inside.

"Ship oars!" Black Oak O'Malley bellowed the command. There was a clatter as the sailors raised the long oars out of the

water. When the galley was thirty feet away, Black Oak and a few others jumped into the water and began pulling the ship with ropes. Soon the ship was safe. Still dripping, Black Oak looked around for his wife and daughter.

"Margaret!" he called as he saw his wife running down the path from the castle to the beach. They hugged.

"Where's our Grace?" Black Oak asked, looking around.

"Right here, Father."

A small yelp shot into the air as Grace's mother cried out and then covered her mouth. Her eyes grew wide in shock.

"Grace!" Her father stood still and looked at his daughter. "Grace!" he cried. "Did the Wee Folk get hold of you and cut your hair?" He grinned.

As soon as he grinned, Grace knew it was all right.

"No, I cut it myself, Father. I want to go

to sea." She turned to her mother. "And now you need not call me a lady ever more."

"*Grainne Mhaol,*" whispered her father. In the Gaelic language that means Grace the Bald. Then both her parents began to laugh. They hugged and kissed her stubbly head and said, "Grainne Mhaol," over and over until the name became sweet as music.

Chapter 3

To Capture a Star

Grace did not sleep. She would not sleep. She could not sleep. It was, after all, her first voyage. Black Oak had set her on the midnight watch. When it finished, well before daybreak, she stayed on deck. She wanted to see the dawn. She looked out over the sea to its rosy edge. Without a breath of wind to ripple the water, it stretched still and smooth before her.

"It is like Mananan's cape," she whispered to her father. There was an old story about the sea lord's great cloak. It could reflect every color, just like the sea did. It was this cloak that he spread around the island of Eire, or Ireland, to keep it from enemies.

Black Oak now looked toward the Isle of Man, where, the legend said, Mananan lived. "Well, as much as I am happy for Mananan's protection, I wish he would lift his cloak and let a wisp of wind slip through."

"You wouldn't need the wind if you had the sea lord's ship, *Ocean Sweeper*."

Black Oak laughed. "That would be nice, now wouldn't it, Grace? A magic ship that needed neither oar nor sail, but only the thoughts of its captain to move her."

Stories of the magic ships were Grace's favorites. She thought that if she ever had a ship of her own, she would call it *Ocean Sweeper*.

The sails of the galley flapped lazily.

For this trip Black Oak had taken a larger ship, powered by much bigger square sails.

Grace had been very excited when she found out that her first sea voyage would be aboard such a ship. It meant they were going far, as far as France or Spain.

"Grace, plant your feet wider to steady yourself, and press the cross-staff hard to your brow." Black Oak was teaching his daughter how to find her way across the sea using the sky as a map.

This was *much* harder than spinning, Grace thought. She had taken the position of the North Star before, on a calm, windless night. But she had never tried to do it on a windy night like this. The deck of the ship bucked, tossed by the churning waves. Now the North Star skittered about like a frisky lamb dancing across a meadow. Except this meadow was the night sky, and a hard rain had begun to fall.

She only had a few minutes to get the star's position. Soon the rain would blot out every star in the sky, Grace's face was wet and she could not see well, but she knew she could do this.

"Don't help me!" she yelled as a sailor tried to steady her. "I can do it myself," she muttered. She hated it when the others treated her like a baby. She was no baby—she was as tough as the rest of them. She just needed the chance to prove it.

Anyway, a person did not need big muscles to get a star fix. It was not like pulling up an anchor or pulling in a huge flapping sail about to tear loose in a gale wind. Still, it would have helped if she had been taller. She had to stand on tiptoe to see over the gunwales with the cross-staff. She bit her lip and pressed the cross-staff hard to her brow, just the way her father had told her. She must fix that star, and once the star was captured in the marks of the crosspiece, they would know where they were in this vast sea. It was not magic. It was science. It was math. It made sense out of a vast and complicated place. Grace liked that.

The sailors who learned this science became pilots and captains on her father's other ships. Those who did not were left with the least interesting tasks. But everything on a ship at sea was more interesting than churning butter or spinning wool on land.

"Got it!" she cried. "Mark twelve!" In a firm voice she called out the sight mark on the cross-staff. Her father smiled as she lowered it. She had pressed it so hard against her forehead that a dent had been left in the skin. She rubbed her hand over the mark. She didn't mind. After all, she had captured a star!

By the end of her first voyage, Grace had learned most of the skills of a seaman. She was just as quick to learn how to gamble. She became so good at playing cards and dice that the sailors gave her a new nick-name: *Grainne-na-gCearbhach,* Grace the Gambler.

She played hard and she played fair and she played to win. This was how Grace did everything on her father's ship. During those first voyages Black Oak was very proud of his daughter.

Chapter 4

Mad Dogs and Merrows

Too dark to throw the chip now," said Black Oak O'Malley. By dropping a wood chip into the water at the bow and then counting the seconds until it passed the stern, he could figure the speed of the ship. Then over time he could tell how far they had sailed.

"Suppose so," Grace said. They were on another voyage now. She had learned much, but still had more that she wanted to try. She leaned over the rail and looked deep into the dark water. Then a thought came to her. It might be too dark to see the chip, but not too dark to climb the rigging. Just a few days before, she had vowed to climb the rigging when there was a real wind blowing. On earlier voyages she had been aloft only when the seas were calm. But she knew that a real sailor could do the same tasks in calm weather or in a storm when the wind was howling and the seas tossing. The wind had been picking up on this evening. Hadn't her father just said that it looked like Lord Mananan was fixing up a smart gale for them?

She knew that if she asked, her father would never let her aloft during the full blast of a gale. If she was nearly too short to capture a star, her father would think she was much too light to wrestle with the wind in the rigging. But what if she got aloft before he could say no? She would already be there when the first order to shorten sail was called.

Hiding in the shadows at the foot of the mast, she waited until no one was about. When it was clear, she began to climb the ratlines. Within a minute she was at the crosstrees. She looked down. The waves broke round the ship like packs of mad dogs with mouths foaming, biting and tearing at the ship as it sliced through the sea. The wind smashed into Grace's face. Wrapping her arms tighter around the mast, she set her foot on the next rope step in the ratlines. She felt if she went high enough, she just might touch a star. Something thrilled in the deepest part of her soul. She loved this mad-dog sea, this wild wind, and this sky of sliding stars.

"Aloft!" the cry came, and not a moment too soon. The sails seemed ready to split in the punch of the wind.

There was a mighty oath from below as

her father picked out the small figure of his daughter against the sky.

"Who let her up there! Who? I shall cut out his tongue and feed it to the sharks!"

"No one, Da! I let myself up," Grace shouted as loudly as she could, but the words were torn from her mouth by the wind. Soon a sailor appeared, a knife bright between his teeth. "You hang on, lassie, 'cause if you fall, someone else will die, too!" The words hissed out like hot steam over the knife's blade. "Just remember that the next time you decide to do a fool thing like climbing up here." Grace felt terrible—for about five seconds. Then the sailor added, " 'Tis no place for a girl up here!"

"I'll prove you wrong," she said in a husky voice. "I'll prove you wrong."

She did. She was soon creeping out along the footropes that followed the yard that fitted across the mast and held the sails. When sail had to be taken in, it was raised and tied to the yards with ropes. Grace had to be careful, because a snapping sail could slice a face wide open or, worse yet, knock a person into the sea.

The wind had not been this strong when Grace had climbed up. But now she was here. And yet if she were to be a true sailor, she must do more than just hang on. She must work. The sailor next to her was wrestling with an armful of sailcloth. She did have her rope. But dare she let go with one hand to grab it from round her waist? She slung her whole arm as far around the yard as she could. She felt something snap at her forehead. It stung terribly. Grace closed her eyes and prayed for strength. She reached for the rope. Holding one end of the rope in her teeth, she reached around for the loose end. It whipped and twisted like a snake, but finally she caught it. She crept to where the sailor had a bunch of sail held against the yard.

"Good!" he gasped. "Now tie a half-hitch knot, then another." She did it—she didn't know how, but she did it. The sailor was soon handing her another rope. "Follow me, lassie. We'll tame these merrows yet!"

"Merrows! I thought merrows were kindly water fairies."

"Ah, that they be, the ones that live in the lakes and rivers," the sailor said. "But here on the sea 'tis opposite. The freshwater fairy ladies are beautiful. Their men are ugly with green hair and pig snouts and red glowing eyes. But the salty-sea merrows, the women that is, they be as ugly as the men merrows of the lake. They must be growing quite jealous of you. Afraid their handsome men merrows will run off with a pretty lass like yourself."

"You're silly," Grace said. But she realized that even in this gale she had grown calm enough to listen to a story and tie knots as they worked along the yard.

"You think I be silly, do you? Well, where do you think that blood on the sail you just tied came from?"

There was blood on the cloth and on the rope as well. "I don't know," she said.

"From your own forehead. The little merrow fairies are set on making you as ugly as them. They want to slice up your pretty face." Then Grace remembered the rope snapping against her head. Now she felt something wet running down the side of her face. She slid her tongue out of the corner of her mouth and tasted her own warm blood. They won't get me again, she vowed to herself.

Chapter 5

Grace the Pirate

Wish the fog was a bit thicker." Grace and Donal, the sailor with whom she had worked on the rigging, were now on deck, looking out from the shadows under the sea cliffs of an island in Clew Bay. The galley had tucked into the sea cave to wait for an English ship—a ship heavy with damask and silk, wine and spices to be traded in Galway, where the O'Malleys and other clans were forbidden to trade.

"Get you a pretty piece of silk, Grace,

and one for your Mam, too!" Donal winked, his eye flashing blue through the darkness of the cave.

"How do you know there'll be silk, Donal?"

"You'll remember this ship, a caravel. Same one we piloted around Slyne Head two months past. We knew they'd be coming back. The captain is a real blabbermouth! This will teach him to brag about trading cargo."

Grace opened her eyes in wonder.

"You think it's all just seafaring, don't you? Sailing the breezes with skill and wits, and climbing the rigging," Donal said.

Grace nodded.

"Well, it isn't." He paused. "It's listening, too! And having a keen eye that measures the length of the vessel and counts the men and the guns, and knows where they store the gunpowder and where they keep torches and the cargo, all while helping these poor blighters sail through the rocky channels."

"You do all that?"

"Yes, when I am the pilot. Then I come back and tell your father everything. And he decides if we should take their cargo next time round."

Black Oak had decided. And tonight was to be the first time Grace would be on board during a raid of a foreign vessel. She had been made to promise three things:

1) to climb into an old wine cask as soon as they began to sail from the cave and to stay there quietly through the entire raid, until told to come out;

2) to obey any order given to her by her father or one of his sailors;

3) and finally, perhaps most important, never to tell her mother she had plundered and pirated with her father.

"They don't know you're doing that when you pilot them?" Grace asked Donal.

"I dare say if they did, they would never hire us in the first place." He paused. "Sssh!" He cupped his hand to his ear. There was a high shrill squeak that sounded exactly like the cry of a fish hawk. But it was not. This was the signal from the scouts. The English vessel was nearing. It was time for Grace to climb in the barrel.

She wasn't sure she wanted to be in a barrel during all the excitement, but she wasn't sure if what was about to happen was right, either. Her father thought so, but her mother didn't.

The men began to row with muffled oars. Sails were raised and the swift little galley, along with three others, glided into the bay. The current was with them. Skirting the fringes of the whirlpool off the island's point, they gained another knot of speed. A breeze kicked up. Grace felt the excitement swell in her throat as the dim outline of the heavy and lumbering English merchant vessel melted from the fog.

When she peeked out from the barrel later, they were alongside the ship. A rope

snaked through the fog. Then another and another. At the end of each rope was the iron claw known as a grappling hook. The galley rocked as a dozen or more men swung out on the lines now attached to the English vessel and clambered aboard with swords drawn. Her father was among them. She heard his voice rumble, "Give over your cargo at once. Spare your vessel and your lives by quick action. You are at our mercy."

Suddenly four or more of her father's galleys appeared out of the fog. Their torches were ablaze now, the sailors ready to pitch them onto the deck of the merchant ship.

There was a sudden and awful cry. Then the clash of metal against metal. Grace was aware of a sharp odor of rope and tar burning. She peeked out. There were great billows of smoke pouring from the merchant vessel and then a spurt of flames. Through the fiery red light and the black of the smoke she saw the glint of swords. She felt someone pushing her down into the barrel. It was Donal. "Fools, they are!" He swore. She felt the galley rock violently. Dare she peek again? Midst the hollers and the flapping sails she heard the yelp of a dog. Before she knew it there was a furry wriggling mop of a thing stuffed down on top of her head. Then something wet and warm trickled down her cheek. "You're wetting me!"

Her father's face peered down. "Be kind to the little fellow. I just killed his English master." His face vanished. She heard him bellow again. "All right, lads, that's the last of the cargo we can get. She'll explode when the fire reaches the gunpowder. Row now!"

A few minutes passed. Another command. "Set sail! We're free and clear."

And Grace was cozy in her barrel cuddling her new treasure that was as precious as all the wine and silk and damask her father had just plundered.

Chapter 6

Grace in Battle

Grace had sailed several voyages during her first two years of going to sea with her father. But never had there been so much fog as on this one. Sound turns queer in the fog. Grace remembered thinking that as she lay in her hammock with her new dog just before her watch. The rigging moans, and sometimes the creaking timbers of the hull sound like the mewling of a cat. The screech of the sea gulls scrapes like a blade on stone.

A rustling of water against the hull made Grace think of the merrows. Were the girl merrows lapping the hull with their twisted tongues, their green hair streaming and pig snouts blowing bubbles? Were they hoping to cut at her face once more? She touched the scar on her head. Sounds cannot be trusted in air milky with fog. But suddenly a shout split the night. "Back the fore topsail!" The ship slowed and began to turn.

It was her father's voice shouting. Then all at once the fog was broken by fire! It was not merrows, but pirates! The ship was under attack. Grace felt it tilt to port. The noise of feet sounded overhead. Her father stuck his head through the deck hatch. "Hide! Grace, hide! In the barrels in the bow." But then the ship rocked violently. Cargo tumbled, and the path to the barrels was blocked. With crates flying about and barrels rolling, it seemed as if Grace might be crushed. She had a clear view through the hatch to the ratlines. She would rather get out and fight than be smashed like a worm by rolling barrels.

Grabbing a dagger, she scrambled up through the hatch and reached for the nearest line. The deck was a writhing mass of fighting men. Daggers were drawn and fire leaped from the sails. She looked down and saw a terrible design painted in blood, smoke, and flames. And then Grace spotted her father, bleeding and stumbling. Behind him she saw the glint of a dagger.

"On your mother's grave!" She screeched a terrible oath and swung down from the rigging, knocking her father's attacker to the deck. In the storm of flames and oaths there was a silence. "It's a maid!" said one Englishman in surprise.

And then Black Oak's sailors remembered too that she was a maid, a child. In truth, the sailors had forgotten over the course of so many voyages that Grace was

still just a young girl with short hair. To them she had become another sailor. She was shorter, perhaps, skinnier, and faster in the rigging, but she could get a good star sight and figure the ship's speed better than most.

When the crew saw what she had done, and watched as she climbed high into the rigging to cut away the burning sails, they fought even harder. It was on that night that they saw what she was to become: Grace O'Malley, Pirate Queen of the Irish Seas.

Within a few years she would command a fleet of over fifty ships with hundreds of men from different clans of Ireland. And her name would be known far beyond the Irish Sea.

Chapter 7

Many Years Later— Two Queens Meet

She is taller than I am, Queen Elizabeth I of England thought as Grace O'Malley was led into the room where the queen met her guests.

She is shorter than I am, Grace thought, and she does not like it.

The two women stood apart. They eyed each other in quiet wonder. One stood with her hair piled and curled, tucked with shining jewels. The other wore a chieftain's cloak over her dress. A knife was slid into her wide belt.

The queen studied Grace. How had this woman come by her power? She, Elizabeth, had inherited a crown and all the rights of a ruler of a state. Grace O'Malley had not. Yet for nearly fifty years Grace had been a great sea captain and commanded a large fleet. She was a pirate and a trader and had broken all the laws, yet still she led and ruled. She had defended her husband's castles from the attacks of English soldiers. She had then been imprisoned in the worst dungeon in Ireland by the English rulers, who wanted to stop her pirating. And yet here she was. Strong and feisty as ever.

Elizabeth smiled to herself when she thought of the letters Sir Richard Bingham, the new English governor of Connaught, had sent to her. He wanted to crush Grace O'Malley. Bingham had never met her, but he hated that she stood in the way of his control of the region. He hated most of all that she was a woman. Bingham had killed one of Grace's sons and captured two other sons and Grace herself in a bloody battle. He had been shamed into letting her go, but he made sure she was left with nothing. He took all of her thousands of cattle and horses. And he took her ships. She had lost not only her power but her means to survive.

Grace walked toward the queen. Am I meeting my saltwater merrow on land? she thought. But this woman had a sharp nose and beady eyes. And her hair was not green, but a strange color of red. They were about to shake hands, but the queen had lifted hers quite high. Grace saw what she was doing. The queen wanted her to reach for her hand. I am taller and I am proud, Grace thought. We are evenly matched in other ways. So Grace, the Pirate Queen of the Irish Seas, bent her knees a little so that she would have to reach for the Queen of England's hand.

The first thing the queen offered Grace was a title. She could be countess, the Countess of Connaught. But Grace shook her head sadly. She wanted no titles. There was a giggle from people in the queen's court. No one had ever heard of someone saying no to a title. But that was just what this wild woman had done.

What Grace wanted were her cattle and horses, her captured sons, and her fleet. To get it back, she made a very clever offer. "I will serve Your Majesty by fighting your enemies in Ireland with my galleys and men. By fire, sword, and sail I promise."

Grace spoke in Latin, for that was the only language that the two women shared. After she spoke, Grace's nose began to run, as it so often did when she was indoors. A lady-in-waiting to the queen gave her a lace handkerchief. Grace blew her nose and then

tossed the hankie in the fire. The ladies of the court gasped.

"We meant the handkerchief to be put in your pocket, not into the fire," one of the ladies said.

Grace turned to her. "In Ireland we have higher standards of cleanliness."

The ladies were amazed at her boldness, but the queen did not flinch. Elizabeth touched her fingertips to her powdered cheeks, which were as white as stone. Her eyes took in everything about this woman standing in her grand court.

How silly her ladies-in-waiting seemed then. And how rare was this old woman. Why should she not have her ships? Why should her sons not have their freedom? And that bully Bingham! What did he know about real bravery?

"I have pity on this aged woman without title and without position," the queen said. Grace tried to look humble. "I grant her land and her herds of cattle and horses. Her sons shall be let go. And since she has promised to fight our enemies, may she be free to do so. Her fleet of galleys shall be given back."

Grace bowed deeply to the queen. She had won! And as she left the queen's room, her nose began to run again. This time she wiped it on her cloak. Fie on those silly lace hankies. She also remembered to walk a bit hunched over, as a poor old lady would.

Author's Note

The Pirate Queen

Grace O'Malley was one of the most fascinating women of her era. In a society where women were mostly confined at home, from an early age she was more interested in fishing and trading than spinning and cooking. She had a fiery, independent spirit that made a deep impression on everyone she met. This is clear from how often her name is mentioned in letters and state documents. She was shrewd and strong and commanded loyalty from men of many different clans, and respect even from her enemies. Her unusual position as a powerful leader made her the subject of legend and song, but historians of her time did not want to acknowledge that a woman could do all she did.

Grace O'Malley was born in 1530 at a time when Ireland was mostly ruled by clan chieftains under Irish law, although it was an English colony. Even when some chieftains accepted English titles in exchange for loyalty to the crown, clans such as the O'Malleys enjoyed the freedom to make their living by fishing, trading, and pirating. She was married (twice) and had four children, but she still continued to be involved in these activities. (According to one legend, she gave birth to her youngest son during a trading voyage, when Turkish pirates attacked the ship. When she realized the battle wasn't going well, she was forced to stash the baby in a safe place and fight the pirates

herself.) She always knew how to maintain her power on land and sea, playing along with English or Irish rulers to get her way.

Then Sir Richard Bingham became the governor of Connaught. He was determined to enforce English rule in wild western Ireland—and to crush Grace O'Malley. He imprisoned her, took her herds of cattle and horses, impounded her ships, and even killed her son Owen. Facing the wrath of the English governor, and stripped of her wealth and means of support, she had the courage to petition Queen Elizabeth I herself. Although it is not certain what happened at that meeting (the scene described in this book is based on a legend), it is a fact that Queen Elizabeth took pity on the "aging woman" and returned to Grace her fleet of galleys. Grace kept her part of the bargain with the queen and tried to fight England's enemies on land and sea. But she never gave up her independence, and continued to fish, trade, and pirate in and around Clew Bay.

Grace O'Malley was a woman who lived in a man's world, who was trusted by the hundreds of men she commanded. Even though she bargained with the English rulers of Ireland to get her way, she never sacrificed her goal of "maintenance on land and sea." Until her last days Grace O'Malley managed to do what she'd wanted to do since she was a girl: to sail galleys like her father, Black Oak.

If you liked *Grace the Pirate*, look for these books in your library or bookstore:

Behind the Couch by Mordicai Gerstein
When Zachary crawls behind the couch to retrieve a fallen toy, he uncovers a fantasy world and more surprises.

Christopher Davis's Best Year Yet by Lauren L. Wohl
With each change of season, eight-year-old Christopher not only faces new challenges, but new adventures as well.

Eat! by Steven Kroll
Harry Howell's classmates have ridiculed him ever since he became a vegetarian. Will he ever be able to convince his classmates that "fruit is cute"?

The Kwanzaa Contest by Miriam Moore and Penny Taylor
Ron wonders if anyone will think he is as special as his older sister. Then he creates an African symbol of freedom in celebration of Kwanzaa that just might get him noticed.

Mamá's Birthday Surprise by Elizabeth Spurr
When two brothers and their sister concoct a plan to reunite Mamá with her long-lost uncle, their mysterious family hero turns out to be the biggest (and best) surprise of all.

My Sister the Sausage Roll by Barbara Ware Holmes
In her letters, Eloise reports to her father that her baby sister rates a grade C. As her letters continue, will the baby ever improve to an A?

Racetrack Robbery by Ellen Leroe
Ghost Dog is hot on the trail of an action-packed mystery when an impostor shows up at the racetrack.

Spy in the Sky by Kathleen Karr
During the American Civil War, young Ridley Jones gets the chance of a lifetime when he is asked to become a member of the elite Balloon Corps.

If you liked *Grace the Pirate*, look for these books in your library or bookstore:

Behind the Couch by Mordicai Gerstein
When Zachary crawls behind the couch to retrieve a fallen toy, he uncovers a fantasy world and more surprises.

Christopher Davis's Best Year Yet by Lauren L. Wohl
With each change of season, eight-year-old Christopher not only faces new challenges, but new adventures as well.

Eat! by Steven Kroll
Harry Howell's classmates have ridiculed him ever since he became a vegetarian. Will he ever be able to convince his classmates that "fruit is cute"?

The Kwanzaa Contest by Miriam Moore and Penny Taylor
Ron wonders if anyone will think he is as special as his older sister. Then he creates an African symbol of freedom in celebration of Kwanzaa that just might get him noticed.

Mamá's Birthday Surprise by Elizabeth Spurr
When two brothers and their sister concoct a plan to reunite Mamá with her long-lost uncle, their mysterious family hero turns out to be the biggest (and best) surprise of all.

My Sister the Sausage Roll by Barbara Ware Holmes
In her letters, Eloise reports to her father that her baby sister rates a grade C. As her letters continue, will the baby ever improve to an A?

Racetrack Robbery by Ellen Leroe
Ghost Dog is hot on the trail of an action-packed mystery when an impostor shows up at the racetrack.

Spy in the Sky by Kathleen Karr
During the American Civil War, young Ridley Jones gets the chance of a lifetime when he is asked to become a member of the elite Balloon Corps.

Read all the Hyperion Chapters

2ND GRADE

Alison's Fierce and Ugly Halloween by Marion Dane Bauer

Alison's Puppy by Marion Dane Bauer

Alison's Wings by Marion Dane Bauer

The Banana Split from Outer Space by Catherine Siracusa

Edwin and Emily by Suzanne Williams

Emily at School by Suzanne Williams

The Peanut Butter Gang by Catherine Siracusa

Scaredy Dog by Jane Resh Thomas

2ND/3RD GRADE

The Best, Worst Day by Bonnie Graves

I Hate My Best Friend by Ruth Rosner

Jenius: The Amazing Guinea Pig by Dick King-Smith

Jennifer, Too by Juanita Havill

The Missing Fossil Mystery by Emily Herman

Mystery of the Tooth Gremlin by Bonnie Graves

No Room for Francie by Maryann Macdonald

Secondhand Star by Maryann Macdonald

Solo Girl by Andrea Davis Pinkney

Spoiled Rotten by Barthe DeClements

3RD GRADE

Behind the Couch by Mordicai Gerstein

Christopher Davis's Best Year Yet by Lauren L. Wohl

Eat! by Steven Kroll

Grace the Pirate by Kathryn Lasky

The Kwanzaa Contest by Miriam Moore and Penny Taylor

Mamá's Birthday Surprise by Elizabeth Spurr

My Sister the Sausage Roll by Barbara Ware Holmes

Racetrack Robbery by Ellen Leroe

Spy in the Sky by Kathleen Karr

Kathryn Lasky

I grew up in Indiana, about as far from any ocean as one could get. But in our backyard there was a pond. My sister and my best friend and I used to take voyages across this shallow pond in a very small rowboat we named the U.S. *Teacup*. We even tried to rig a sail out of old bedsheets. In our imaginations, the pond became an ocean and the other side of the bank where the muskrats lived was the distant shore of some far-off land. Sometimes we were pirates. We painted our faces and wore bandannas and carried sticks for swords.